HAPPY FEET™
Mumble's Journey

PRICE STERN SLOAN
Published by the Penguin Group
Penguin Group (USA) Inc., 375 Hudson Street, New York, New York 10014, U.S.A.
Penguin Group (Canada), 90 Eglinton Avenue East, Suite 700, Toronto, Ontario,
Canada M4P 2Y3 (a division of Pearson Penguin Canada Inc.)
Penguin Books Ltd, 80 Strand, London WC2R 0RL, England
Penguin Ireland, 25 St Stephen's Green, Dublin 2, Ireland
(a division of Penguin Books Ltd)
Penguin Group (Australia), 250 Camberwell Road, Camberwell, Victoria 3124, Australia
(a division of Pearson Australia Group Pty Ltd)
Penguin Books India Pvt Ltd, 11 Community Centre, Panchsheel Park,
New Delhi - 110 017, India
Penguin Group (NZ), Cnr Airborne and Rosedale Roads, Albany, Auckland 1310,
New Zealand (a division of Pearson New Zealand Ltd)
Penguin Books (South Africa) (Pty) Ltd, 24 Sturdee Avenue, Rosebank,
Johannesburg 2196, South Africa

Penguin Books Ltd, Registered Offices:
80 Strand, London WC2R 0RL, England

Library of Congress Cataloging-in-Publication Data is available.

ISBN 0-8431-2104-1 10 9 8 7 6 5 4 3 2 1

Adapted by Megan E. Bryant

With special thanks to Kathryn Otoshi
for her invaluable editorial guidance.

A PRICE STERN SLOAN JUNIOR NOVEL

PSS!
PRICE STERN SLOAN

Far away, in the deepest, darkest parts of space, spins a blue and green planet covered in cloudy swirls. If you travel to the southernmost region of the planet, you will find a freezing wasteland, completely covered in ice and snow. But it is there, in the coldest conditions imaginable, that you will also find a most remarkable and courageous nation of beings, who every year find renewed strength to hope, love, and sing from their hearts. These are the Emperor penguins, and the singing is their Heartsongs.

One penguin, Norma Jean, sang so beautifully that all the male penguins sang back to her, hoping to become her match. But with so many songs sung all at once, how could Norma Jean ever hear the song that was meant for her?

"Boys, boys, boys!" she exclaimed. "Give a chick a chance!"

Silence fell over Emperor Land. Then a new song rang through the air. Tall, strong, and with a voice that would melt your heart, Memphis moved toward Norma Jean, singing the song that was just for her. She listened, then began her own song in tune with his. And so Norma Jean and Memphis met in the usual way: Their songs became love, and their love became the egg.

But all too soon, Memphis and Norma Jean had to say good-bye. When the egg hatched, their baby would be hungry. So in the tradition of the Emperor penguins, all the mothers left to hunt for fish in the deep waters far away while the fathers took care of their precious eggs.

"If only you could stay, darling," Memphis said sadly.

"There are no fish on the ice, my love," replied Norma Jean. "You've got to stay here to do egg time."

Memphis sighed, but he knew Norma Jean was right. "Give it to me, sugar-pie," he said.

Quickly and carefully, Norma Jean passed the egg to Memphis. It spent only a second on the freezing ice before he tucked it safely into his warm, cozy brood pouch.

"Got it!" Memphis said proudly. "*Whoa!* I think I felt the little buddy move!"

"You gonna be okay, Daddy?" Norma Jean asked. Her voice was full of worry. "Winter is a dangerous time out on the ice . . ."

"Don't you worry about a thing, Norma Jean," Memphis replied. "I'll keep him safe and warm till you get back."

"Bye-bye, now!" Norma Jean called as she joined the group of females. "I'll see you in the spring!"

Memphis watched Norma Jean leave as the first snowflakes of winter drifted around him. With a growing sadness in his heart, he realized just how far away spring really was.

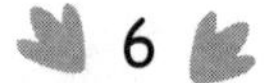

CHAPTER 2

Soon the icy winds swirled as the cold sun was swallowed by the blackness of night. As another brutal winter descended, the father penguins came together with their eggs, huddling to create warmth for all.

Noah the Elder, the leader of the Emperor penguins, raised his voice above the howling winds. "When all others leave . . ." he chanted.

"We remain!" the huddle replied.

"When the sun vanishes . . ." chanted Noah.

"We remain!" answered the huddle.

"Heed the wisdom, brothers," Noah's voice rang out. "Make a huddle and share the cold! Each must take his turn against the icy blast if we are to survive the endless night!"

As the penguins huddled against the freezing

winds a glowing swirl formed above them, creating a vision of the Great Guin filling the ocean with fish!

"Give praise to the Great Guin, who puts songs in our hearts and food in our bellies!" Noah called.

But Memphis was not mindful of the almighty Guin, provider of all. He only had thoughts for his Norma Jean. He could see a vision of her now, singing in her irresistible voice. "Oh, I think I wanna dance now!" he cried, barely aware that he had started shimmying and shaking—dancing—to the memory of Norma Jean's Heartsong.

Then something terrible happened. As Memphis danced, he gave a quick hip-wiggle, and the egg shot out of his brood pouch and slid down the ice!

"*Whoa!* Oh, no! *Noooo!*" cried Memphis, panicking. He raced to rescue the egg, knowing he only had seconds before it froze. After frantically searching, Memphis finally found the egg nestled in a snowdrift, half buried by the swirling snow. Memphis tucked it back into his brood pouch and looked around to see if anyone was watching. "No harm done.

Everything's gonna be just fine," he told himself firmly as he rejoined the huddle. But deep in his heart, Memphis knew the truth: Dropping the egg was the biggest mistake an Emperor penguin could ever make.

Day by day, the harsh winds quieted and the bitter snows softened. At last, the sun returned to the sky. Memphis's long wait through the terrible winter was finally over.

CRACK! Crack! Crack! All across Emperor Land, the eggs were hatching! The fluffy chicks broke out of their shells, blinking at the bright sunlight. Shouts of joy and laughter rang through the air as the fathers met their babies for the first time.

But Memphis stood alone, staring at his egg, waiting for a sign—a crack, a sound from within.

But nothing happened.

"Memphis? Is everything okay?" asked his friend Maurice.

"I . . . I don't know," Memphis replied. "I can't

hear anything." He closed his eyes, trying to shut out the memory of dropping the egg.

Maurice's chick, Gloria, tapped the egg with her beak. *Tap-tap-tap.* "Is it empty?" she asked. "Can I have it?"

"Gloria! Stop that!" scolded Maurice.

"That's okay, Maurice," Memphis said miserably, looking at the gray, lifeless egg at his feet.

"These things happen sometimes," Maurice said quietly.

Gloria's little beak tapped the egg again. *Tap-tap-tap.*

Then suddenly . . . the egg tapped back!

Tap-tap-tappity-tap-tap!

Memphis froze. "Wait! Did you hear that?" he exclaimed. "I can hear you, little buddy. Pappy's here! Oh, he's okay, Maurice!" Memphis was relieved!

"Whoaaaa!" Memphis jumped back as one foot popped out of the egg, then another. It rocked and rolled until it flipped over. The two tiny feet landed on the ground, stumbling around all over the ice in a

strange, giddy hippity-hop.

"That's . . . uh . . . different," Memphis said. "*Whoa*, little buddy, slow down!"

"Come back, Mister Mumble!" Gloria giggled at the muffled noises coming from inside the egg.

"Little Mumble—I like that!" Memphis said. "Slow down there, Mumble!"

But the running egg was out of control! It zoomed down the slope and then up the side of an ice wall at top speed. The egg briefly became airborne before crashing straight to the ground. *CRACK!* The egg shattered into hundreds of pieces, and little Mumble was born.

"You okay, son?" Memphis called.

"Ow! Freezy! Fuh-fuh-freezy!" Mumble said as he hopped from foot to foot.

"You'll get used to it," replied Memphis. "Come to Daddy!"

Baby Mumble hippity-hopped over the ice as fast as his little feet could carry him. The Emperor penguins had never seen anything like it.

"What do you make of that?" one of the fathers asked.

"A little wobbly in the knees, huh?" said another.

Even Noah and the other Elders had stopped to watch Mumble's strange walk.

"What are you doing, son?" Memphis asked nervously.

"I'm happy, Pa!" Mumble said.

"What are you doing with your feet?"

"They're happy, too!" exclaimed Mumble as he hippity-hopped all over the ice.

"I wouldn't do that around folks, son," Memphis said. "It ain't Penguin!"

Mumble stopped dancing. His feet were silent on the frozen ground. "Okay, Dad," he said.

"Good boy. Now come over here and get warm," Memphis said. As Mumble charged into the cozy space under his father's belly, Memphis looked around anxiously. The other penguins had stopped staring at them—for now.

CHAPTER 3

As spring arrived in Emperor Land, the fathers and chicks eagerly waited for the mothers to return. But as days passed with no sign of the females, the penguins began to worry.

"What's keeping them?" asked Eggbert the Elder.

"I hope it's not a fish shortage," replied Noah darkly.

But in the crowd of waiting fathers, Memphis had his own worries. What would Norma Jean do when she saw Mumble's strange walk? He turned to his son. "Do you remember what I told you?" Memphis asked. "About what to do when you see your mama?"

"I stand perfectly still!" Mumble said. "But how will I know which one is Mama?"

"Oh, you'll know, all right," Memphis replied. "She's got a wiggle in her walk, and a giggle in her talk, and a song so sweet, it'll break your heart."

"*Wives-ho! Wives-ho!*" a voice boomed across the land. Others joined in, pointing at the distant figures on the horizon. The mama penguins had returned at last!

Before Memphis could stop him, Mumble rushed toward the mamas—and was lost in the crowd of penguins!

"Mumble! Mumble! Get back here" Memphis yelled frantically. All over Emperor Land, families were being reunited. But Memphis searched frantically through the crowd for his son and mate.

"Memphis!" A familiar voice, sweet as honey, carried across the ice. It was the moment Memphis had been waiting for—his Norma Jean had returned! But how could he face her without their baby?

"Norma Jean!" Memphis called as he hurried to her.

"Oh, Daddy!" she exclaimed. "Where's the baby?"

"Well, honey," began Memphis. "I'll . . . ah . . . find him!"

"You *lost* the baby?" Norma Jean asked, shocked.

"I'll find him—don't worry!" Memphis said.

"Mama! Mama!" shouted a tiny voice from across the icy plain.

"No, stay! We'll come to you!" Memphis called to Mumble.

But it was too late. Little Mumble was so excited that he started hippity-hopping to his mother as fast as his feet could carry him—forgetting all about the promise he'd made to Memphis.

"What's wrong with his feet?" Norma Jean exclaimed.

"Oh . . . uh . . . he'll grow out of it," stammered Memphis.

Mumble ran to his mama and hugged her leg.

They laughed as they twirled around the ice. Norma Jean looked adoringly at her son. She didn't mind that Mumble was a little different. He was absolutely perfect just the way he was.

"Oh, Memphis!" Norma Jean cried, cuddling her son. "He's gorgeous!"

"Isn't he, though?" Memphis said with relief.

"Open up, sweetie," Norma Jean said. "Mama has a little something for you." After she fed Mumble some of the small fish she had caught, Norma Jean looked at Memphis. "It looks like we'll be facing a lean season, Daddy," she said quietly. "We had to search far and wide to find fish this year."

"Aw, baby, I'm not worried," Memphis replied. "As long as we're together, everything's gonna be just fine."

Surrounded by his parents' love, little Mumble grew. Soon he was big enough to start school at Penguin Elementary while his parents took turns making the long trip to the ocean to hunt for fish.

"Good morning, class," Miss Viola said. "Today we begin with the most important lesson you will ever learn. Does anyone know what that is?"

Seymour, the largest toddler in the class, took a guess. "Fishin'?"

Miss Viola shook her head. "No, I'm afraid not," she said. "Mumble?"

"Um, don't eat yellow snow?" Mumble guessed hopefully.

"No, that's not it, either," Miss Viola replied.

"It's our Heartsong, Miss," Gloria piped up.

"Excellent, Gloria! Without our Heartsong, we can't be truly Penguin, can we?" asked Miss Viola.

"No!" all the chicks replied together, shaking their heads.

"But my dears—it's not something I can actually teach you," continued Miss Viola. "Does anyone know why?"

"You can't teach it to us, ma'am, because we have to find our Heartsongs all by ourselves," Gloria said

proudly. "It's the voice you hear inside—the voice of who you truly are."

"Exactly, Gloria! Now, let's all be very still. Take a moment—and let it come to you," Miss Viola encouraged the class.

For a moment, the baby penguins were quiet. Then they all started chattering at once.

"Me! Pick me!"

"I'm ready! I've got one!"

"One at a time, one at a time!" Miss Viola laughed. "Seymour, let's start with you."

Seymour strutted up to Miss Viola. He started rapping in a raspy voice, bouncing in rhythm to the beat.

"Yes, I like that one!" Miss Viola said. "I could really get jiggy with it!"

"I'm ready!" Gloria exclaimed. "I've got one!"

"Ahh, I thought you might, Gloria," Miss Viola said. "Go ahead."

Gloria started to sing in a clear, sweet voice. Mumble had never heard anything so wonderful in

all his life. All over Emperor Land, penguins stopped to listen to her powerful Heartsong.

"That was beautiful!" Mumble exclaimed when Gloria stopped singing.

"Mumble, why don't you share your Heartsong," suggested Miss Viola.

"Okay!" Mumble said as he skipped to the front of the class. "Mine's . . . um . . . boom-boom-boom ssssssshhhhh, chippita-chippita-whishhhhh! BOOM!"

The baby penguins started to snicker.

Miss Viola looked confused. "You heard *that* in your heart?" she asked. "My dear, that's not even a tune."

"It's not?" asked Mumble.

"Not at all, my dear," replied Miss Viola. "A tune sounds like this: La-la-la-la-la-la-la!"

"Oh. Okay," Mumble said. He took a deep breath and tried again. "LalaaaaLAAHHHlalaaa-laaahhhh-*laaAAAAALAAA*!" His tuneless voice screeched over the ice, shattering the peace of Emperor Land. Even Noah and the other Elders took note of

the young penguin whose voice was so unpleasant. And all the chicks laughed loudly at Mumble—except for one.

"Stop it! Stop laughing!" Gloria said angrily. "It's not funny!"

"It's not funny in the least," Miss Viola said gravely. "A penguin without a Heartsong . . . is hardly a penguin at all."

Miss Viola did not delay. She spoke to Mumble's parents as soon as class ended. "His voice—I've never heard anything like it . . ." she said, confused. "And the two of you having such fine voices. To be honest, it's just bizarre. Did anything happen during early development?"

Memphis paused. The memory of dropping Mumble's egg came flooding back—but how could he ever admit what he'd done? In that instant, Memphis made another terrible mistake by choosing to cover up the truth. "Yeah, everything was just fine," he muttered. "It was a tough winter, I

guess, and . . . uh . . . he did hatch a little late . . ."

"I see," Miss Viola said with a heavy sigh.

"To think that my little Mumble might spend his life alone!" worried Norma Jean. "Never to meet his one true love . . ."

The thought was too much for Memphis to bear. "Oh, please, Miss Viola," he said desperately. "Isn't there anything we can do?"

Miss Viola paused. "There is always Mrs. Astrakhan. If anyone can help, Mrs. Astrakhan can!" she encouraged, pointing to a large ice cave in the distance.

Mumble began private singing lessons with Mrs. Astrakhan that very day.

"Can't sink? Can't *sink*? Rubbeesh, darlink!" Mrs. Astrakhan declared. "Every little pengvin has a sonk in his heart!"

Nearby, Memphis and Norma Jean exchanged a hopeful glance. Surely if Mrs. Astrakhan believed Mumble could sing, it was possible!

Mumble was eager to learn. He hung on every word Mrs. Astrakhan said.

"First, you must find a feelink," the famed singing coach instructed. "Happy feelink, sad feelink—maybe *lonely* feelink. You feel it?"

Mumble nodded. "I do!" he said excitedly.

"Good! Now let it out! Be spontaneous!"

Mumble closed his eyes and got ready to sing. But instead of singing, his feet started tapping. He couldn't keep them still! *Tip-tap-tap-tap-tappity-tappity-tap!*

"Vhat? Vhat is that?" asked Mrs. Astrakhan, confused at the sound of Mumble's feet.

Mumble looked up to see his parents and teacher looking very concerned. "I'm being *spontan-uous,*" Mumble explained, stumbling over the big word.

"No, no, no, no, darlink!" Mrs. Astrakhan exclaimed. "You vant to meet beautiful girl? You vant to make the egg?"

"Oh, yes," Mumble said earnestly.

"Then *sink*!" Mrs. Astrakhan encouraged him.

"No more jiggy-jog! Forget body and look deep inside *soul*! Find enormous feelink—so enormous it fills whole body. It must escape or you *explode*!"

Mumble stood very still, listening to his heart. He lifted his head. His eyes were shining; his whole body was shaking.

"Come on, little buddy," whispered Memphis. "You can do it!"

"Yes!" Mrs. Astrakhan exclaimed. "Open your leetle beak . . . and . . . *now*!"

Mumble took a deep breath. He closed his eyes and listened deep within himself. Warmth from his heart spread through his body, from his head all the way down to his feet. In a sudden burst of movement, Mumble's feet started flying across the ice, tapping out amazing rhythms that spread joy through every inch of his body. Never in his life had Mumble felt such excitement. The song in his heart was finally free!

At last, Mumble stopped. He tried to catch his breath. *I did it!* he thought, gasping triumphantly.

But when he turned around, Mumble saw something strange: Mrs. Astrakhan collapsed against an ice block. "Disaster!" she cried. "I never fail before! Never!"

Mumble just shrugged. He didn't understand how dancing could bring him such happiness but upset everyone else. And Memphis was more than upset after the lesson failed. He stormed off angrily as Mumble and Norma Jean ran after him.

"I told you, I never want to see that thing with the feet again!" shouted Memphis, wondering deep down if Mumble's problems were all *his* fault.

"Well, I thought it was kinda cute!" Norma Jean said, interrupting Memphis. "So what if he's a little different? I like different!"

"He's not different!" Memphis exploded. "He's a regular Emperor penguin, and he's got to learn to behave like one!"

"I have an idea!" Mumble spoke up. "I can leave school and stay with you guys!"

"*Whoa, whoa, whoa,*" Memphis said. "You ain't

going nowhere until you've got an education. You're gonna stay in school until you get them singing muscles big and strong, you hear?"

"I'll try, Pa," Mumble promised.

"That's right," said Memphis. "Remember, the word *triumph* starts with 'try' and ends with '*umph*'!" he said, emphasizing the last word with a quick move of his hips.

"Umph," mimicked Mumble, intrigued with his dad's cool hip move. *"Umph, umph, umph!"*

CHAPTER 4

But Mumble couldn't ignore the longing in his heart. He had to dance again. So nearly every day, Mumble slipped out of class and found a place where he could be alone—a place where he could dance away from the watchful eyes of his community and the mocking laughter of his class-mates.

One day, Mumble was so caught up in dancing that he didn't even notice the dark shadow that passed overhead. Suddenly, in the middle of one of Mumble's spins, a menacing grin stopped Mumble in his tracks.

"*Whoa!*" Mumble yelled, jumping backward.

"Whatcha doin' dere, flipper-bird?" asked a mean-looking skua bird. More skuas landed behind the leader, forming a pack.

"Nothing," Mumble said. "What are *you* doing?"

"Oh, I just dropped in for a little lunch," the skua leader said hungrily.

"There's food? Here?" Mumble asked excitedly.

"Dere's food, all right," he said mockingly as the other skuas laughed. "Hmm . . . leg or wing?"

"What? No, not me!" Mumble exclaimed. "I'm a penguin!"

"Exactly!" the skua cackled as he pinned Mumble to the ground with his sharp, curved talons. "De flipper-birds—dat's *you*—eat de fish. De flyin'-birds—dat's *me*—eat de flipper-birds *and* de fish. And lately, dere ain't a lot of fish—so . . ." The skua lunged forward.

"Wait!" Mumble cried in an attempt to distract the skua. He pointed at a yellow band on the skua's leg. "What's that?"

The other skuas groaned. "No! No! Don't get him started! Not dat same old story again!"

But it was too late. The skua leader's eyes lit up as he lifted his foot off of Mumble. "I got two

words for ya—Alien Abduction!" he exclaimed. "Dere's somethin' out there—bigger than us, and smarter, with flat, flabby faces and no beaks! Dey grabbed me and tied me up and strapped me down. Dey poked me with a pointy thing and den—black-out! The next thing I knew, I woke up with this thing on my leg!"

"Did they try to eat you?" asked Mumble, wide-eyed.

"Nah. I guess my pitiful cries for moicy appealed to their better nature," the skua replied.

"Can *I* appeal to your better nature?" Mumble asked hopefully.

"Nice try, kid," the skua laughed. "But no."

As the skuas lurched forward Mumble stumbled backward. "No . . . no . . . *whoaaa!*" he cried, falling into a small crack between two ice ledges. He cowered in a corner, just out of reach.

"Get outta there, flipper-bird!" howled the outraged skuas. They frantically tried to peck Mumble but only managed to get small bits of fluff. Angrily, they flew away, leaving Mumble shaken and alone—but alive.

From that moment on, Mumble never danced by himself again. He knew it was too dangerous to leave the safety of Emperor Land. So Mumble returned to school and sat in the back of the class, where he passed the hours by daydreaming. But still he wondered about the Aliens. What fabulous creatures and strange worlds lay far beyond the ice? Could one small penguin ever hope to know?

The days melted into weeks, and the young penguins grew. Soon they were teenagers, ready to graduate from school. But for Mumble, there would be no ceremony. He had never learned to sing like the rest of his classmates—so Noah the Elder had refused to let him graduate. His peers stood tall and elegant with their sleek black-and-white feathers. But Mumble still had not shed his patchy, soft gray fluff from childhood.

"Who's to say my boy can't graduate?" Norma

Jean asked indignantly. "We can have our own ceremony!"

"You mean it, Ma?" Mumble asked hopefully.

"Norma Jean!" exclaimed Memphis. "Shhh!"

But she paid no attention. "Excelsi-yah!" she cried, throwing bits of fluff in the air.

"Yah-yah-yah!" Mumble cheered with her, and reluctantly, Memphis did, too.

"You go get 'em, tiger!" Norma Jean called out. Mumble hurried to catch up to the other graduates on their way to the sea.

"Remember Stranger Danger," Memphis said nervously. "Watch out for Leopard seals. And killer whales!"

Mumble's unofficial graduation had not gone unnoticed. From the ridge, the Elders watched him hippity-hopping into the distance. "I knew it from the start," Eggbert muttered to Noah. "That boy was always a bad egg. I'm telling you, no good will come of this!"

Meanwhile, Mumble found his classmates

standing at the edge of the glacier squabbling over who should jump into the water. No one wanted to be the first to take the plunge . . .

Except Mumble! "Coming through!" he cried as he dove into the shimmering water. "What are you waiting for? The water's fantastic!"

That was all the other penguins needed to hear. They dove after Mumble, hollering and splashing as they hit the water. The sleek young penguins were expert swimmers—it was almost as if they could fly underwater. Their black-and-white markings camouflaged them perfectly as they sliced through the water at top speeds.

One penguin stood out among the rest: Gloria. She had grown into a sleek and beautiful penguin, and all the males wanted to spend time with her—including Mumble. As the penguins began to head to the surface Mumble followed Gloria, shooting out of the water and slamming into her on the slippery ice!

"*Whoa!* Gloria!" Mumble exclaimed as he skidded on the ice. "I'm sorry. I didn't mean to—"

"Mumble?" Gloria asked. As she tried to steady herself Gloria started slipping, too.

"Coming through!" yelled Seymour as he barreled into Mumble and Gloria, knocking them back into the water.

Mumble swam toward Gloria, trying to find the courage to talk to her. "Uh . . . hi, Gloria," Mumble stammered. "All my life, I wanted to say that you're so—"

"Fish?" Gloria asked.

"Uh . . . yeah," Mumble replied, confused. "You're so . . . fish."

"No, no!" Gloria laughed excitedly. "FISH!" She pointed to a tiny school of fish swimming nearby!

There was chaos in the water as the penguins zoomed after the fish. Though there was not nearly enough for the hundreds of penguins, Mumble managed to catch one. "Gloria! Did you get one?" he asked.

Gloria shrugged off her disappointment. "Nope. Not this time."

"You can have mine," Mumble said immediately.

"Thank you, Mumble, but it's yours," Gloria replied kindly.

"But I *want* you to have it," Mumble insisted.

Whoosh! In a flash, a sneaky skua bird swooped down and snatched the fish from Mumble's mouth! Mumble torpedoed out of the water, grabbing the fish as the skua flew off. Two more skuas latched on; flapping their wings madly, they carried the fish and Mumble into the sky! Mumble held on with all his might, determined to get the fish back and give it to Gloria. The skuas tried to fly higher, but Mumble's weight dragged them down. Suddenly, the fish tore in two, and Mumble plummeted to the ice, hitting the glacier full force—with half the fish still in his beak!

The penguins crowded around Mumble, whose face was buried in the ice. They waited—but Mumble did not move.

"Is he breathing?" one of them asked.

"Mumble?" Gloria asked anxiously as she hurried

to his side. "Are you okay?"

"Take the fish," he muttered, exhausted. "It's for you."

"No, I—"

"*Please* take the fish!" Mumble insisted.

And in that moment it was clear to Gloria that Mumble was truly special. She daintily swallowed the fish. "*Mmmm*, delicious. Thank you, Mumble," she said gratefully.

"You're welcome," Mumble sighed.

That night, at the top of a tall glacier, the young adults gathered to continue celebrating their graduation. Tiny stars twinkled above while the shimmering, glimmering Southern Lights flickered in the frosty sky. The penguins swayed back and forth as Gloria, the starlet of the night, sang one of the loveliest songs they'd ever heard.

Mumble was overcome by the pure beauty of her voice. Barely aware of himself, he lifted his head to the sky and began to sing along. "AaaHHH-

Hyeeeeee-HEEEEEE-haaaaahhhhh-wooooooooooo!"

The concert screeched to a stop.

"Keep it down, weirdo!" one of the penguins yelled.

"What's wrong with you?" added another.

Gloria's kind voice rose above the catcalls. "Mumble," she said gently, "maybe you'd better just . . . you know . . . listen."

"Yeah, I know," Mumble said quietly. "Um . . . sorry, everybody."

Mumble turned and trudged away until he found an ice raft floating in the ocean. It was only big enough for himself—but Mumble didn't mind. He knew that no one would be joining him. He could still hear Gloria's voice echoing across the water. Mumble closed his eyes and listened, knowing that at least now he could enjoy her song without ruining it for anyone else.

Mumble spent that long, lonely night alone, eventually falling into a dreamless sleep as the ice raft drifted into the night.

CHAPTER 5

By the next morning, the ocean currents had carried Mumble's ice raft far from Emperor Land. As the sun began to burn off the early morning mist Mumble was awakened by a harsh jolt. "Cut it out, guys," he mumbled sleepily, thinking that some of the other penguins were playing a trick on him. *Wham!* Another jolt knocked the ice. Mumble opened his eyes and looked down into the water. Something was coming up to the surface fast! Suddenly, a ferocious Leopard seal leaped out of the water, snapping his strong jaws and sharp teeth at Mumble! The Leopard seal was fierce—and wanted Mumble for breakfast. The Leopard seal overturned the ice raft, toppling Mumble into the sea. Mumble swam as fast as he could, using his flippers to fly underwater. But even at his fastest,

the hungry Leopard seal was right behind him!

Snap! The Leopard seal's vicious jaws closed around Mumble's tail. Mumble wriggled free, losing only a few tail feathers. Enraged, the Leopard seal lunged again.

Far away, Mumble saw a light. It was a tunnel of ice in the water—his only chance to escape. He swam faster and faster—the Leopard seal's jaws snapping behind him all the way—and torpedoed through the tunnel of ice straight for the surface. *Whoosh!* Mumble exploded out of the tunnel into the fresh open air and landed gracefully on a glacier.

"*Whoaaaaaa!* Goal!"

"Safe!"

"You da bomb, bro!"

"That's a 9.8!"

"I give you a 10!"

Mumble turned around to see five little Adelie penguins cheering for him. They were small in size but big on attitude! The Adelies were short and squat and loud and boisterous—completely different from the Emperor penguins that Mumble knew. The Adelies weren't about to let anything get them down—not when life could be so much fun. And they'd never pass up the opportunity to make fun of a big, fat, beached Leopard seal!

In the water the Leopard seal was sleek and fast, but on land he was a great, lumbering oaf. The Adelies taunted the Leopard seal, who finally retreated back to the water, defeated. Mumble *tap-tap-tappity-tapped* in triumph. His dancing stopped the Adelies cold.

"Hey, *amigo*, do that again!" one of the Adelies said, impressed. "That clickety-clickety thing with the feet!"

"This?" Mumble asked, showing off a few fancy moves.

"Oh yeah! Oh yeah!" the Adelies cheered. "We like it, Tall Guy!"

The Adelies began to climb a snow-covered hill, trying to tap just like Mumble. Mumble watched them leave—until one of the Adelies called out, "Ain't you coming, Tall Boy?"

Ramon, their leader, added, "You got something better to do?"

Mumble looked back across the water to his home—a place where other penguins never asked him to join in. "No," he replied as he turned away from Emperor Land.

"Well then, come on down to Adelie Land!" Ramon called.

Adelie Land was like no place Mumble had ever been. Thousands of tiny Adelies were everywhere he looked—laughing, jumping, and partying! Mumble towered above them. But the Adelies didn't mind that Mumble was so different. In fact, they liked him *because* he was different!

As Mumble followed the Adelies he tried to keep up with their chatter and figure out who was who. Ramon was clearly the leader—he was certain that he was the coolest, best-looking Adelie penguin in

all of Adelie Land. Nestor seemed like the smartest Adelie, and Lombardo was the quiet one. Raul and Rinaldo made up the rest of the group. Even though the Adelies had different styles and personalities, it was obvious that they were best friends.

"Hey, Stretch, you like to party?" asked Ramon.

"Party? I guess so," replied Mumble—who wasn't quite sure what Ramon meant. Emperor penguins didn't party much at all.

"Then stick with us—we practically own the action around here!" Ramon bragged.

"Even though our food chain gone *loco*, we won't stop partying," added Nestor.

Mumble noticed another Adelie hurrying off with a pebble in his beak. "Is that guy eating *rocks*?" Mumble asked.

The Adelies fell over themselves with laughter. "That's no rock, *hombre*," Raul finally explained.

"Yeah! It's a love stone—for building the nest!" added Lombardo. "The one with the most pebbles wins the *chica*—"

"But we don't need no pebbles," Ramon interrupted. "Because we got *personality.* Watch and learn, Tall Boy!"

Ramon and the Adelies started calling out to a group of female penguins nearby. "Hey, hey, chicky-baby! Watch *this*!" The Adelies broke into a wild flurry of the tapping they had just learned from Mumble.

The chicas were impressed. "Do it again, baby!" one of them said. "Show me those feet."

But Ramon and his pals pretended to be bored. "Nah, I don't feel like it," Ramon said. "Some other time, maybe."

As the chicas walked off in a huff Ramon winked at Mumble. "Leave them wanting more, you know?" Ramon said. "Hold back until mating season, then show them what you got."

"Because either you got it—or not!" Rinaldo said. "And the Amigos—"

"We got it!" the Adelies yelled as they danced a few steps and struck a pose.

Mumble was impressed. "Wow!" he exclaimed. "You think I could get some of it?"

Ramon stopped. "Let me tell something to you. Except for me, Tall Boy, you got the most charisma of anybody!"

Mumble beamed. That was the nicest thing anyone had ever said to him.

"Put that ego away!" Raul teased Ramon. "You gonna hurt someone!"

"Yeah, your big penguin head is blocking the sun," added Lombardo.

But Ramon didn't pay any attention to them. "Oh, you're so jealous," he replied. "I hear people wanting something—*me*!" Ramon began to dance, and the Adelies formed a conga line behind him. "Come on, Stretch!" Ramon yelled to Mumble. "You better join in now!"

Mumble beamed as he jumped into the conga line. "Mambo!" he yelled along with the Adelies. "Mambo!"

The upbeat rhythm and lively steps of the

mambo came easily to Mumble. He tried out fancier moves as he danced up the ice ridge. The Adelies were so impressed that they pushed Mumble to the front so they could follow his lead. For the first time in his life, Mumble was surrounded by friends.

"Tall Guy has definitely got it!" Rinaldo shouted.

Just then, Mumble turned to show off some flashy steps. He didn't realize that he was dancing on a thin ledge of ice. It cracked beneath his feet, sending him straight down a steep icy slope! "AHH-HHHHHHHHHH!" he screamed.

"That guy is so accidentally cool!" Nestor marveled.

One by one, the little penguins leaped after Mumble. They rocketed down the steep slope, zooming through tunnels and around curves, bumping off icy chunks of glacier along the way. The chunks turned into mountainous sections of moving ice and snow that gathered speed, turning into an . . . *avalanche*! The penguins held on to one another, tobogganing down the slope just ahead of the thundering boulders of ice.

Just when it seemed the avalanche was about to crush them, Mumble and the Adelies catapulted off the edge of the glacier—and dove into the choppy ocean below!

CHAPTER 6

Down, down, down the penguins fell through the water, screaming all the way. Far below, they reached an underwater cathedral of ice that was shrouded in darkness and silence.

"That was *mucho* cool," Rinaldo whispered. "Wanna go again?"

"I think we broke the ride!" Lombardo replied.

"I see a light!" Mumble called. "Look over there!"

"You think that's the exit?" asked Ramon.

"There's only one way to find out," Mumble said. He swam toward it, with the Adelies following right behind him. But before they could reach the light, a lifeless creature with twisting arms and a strange armor covering its body blocked their path. "Have you ever seen the likes of that before?" Mumble asked, awestruck.

"I think it's looking at us!" whispered Raul.

"Whatever it is, it doesn't belong here," Mumble said quietly. Cautiously, he tapped its hard surface. Immediately it moved, creaking and moaning as a nasty jet of black liquid spewed into the water. It gave another tremendous groan and shuddered, then plunged into the unseen depths of the sea—dragging the base of the glacier with it!

The Adelies wasted no time escaping from the powerful whirlpool left behind by the glacier. They swam so quickly that Mumble could barely keep up with them!

"Guys! Hey, guys! Wait!" Mumble called as he frantically swam away. He followed the Adelies onto solid land. "What was that thing? And where did it come from?" Mumble asked. "It's so weird. So . . . alien!"

"Elian? I don't know no Elian," Ramon replied. "And I don't wanna know what that thing was!"

"Why not?" protested Mumble. "We have a mystery on our hands. A mind-boggling mystery!

Amigos, we've got to get to the bottom of this!"

Ramon stopped. "You want answers? Then you got to see Lovelace!"

"Who's Lovelace?" Mumble asked.

"Lovelace is the Gooroo!" Nestor replied. "He got the answer to everything!"

"But first," added Ramon, "you gonna need a pebble!"

The Adelies led Mumble to a tall pillar, where a long line of penguins stretched across the ice as far as Mumble could see. At the very top of the pillar was a huge pile of rocks and a glistening cave filled with sparkly icicles. Inside the cave, hidden from view, stood a shadowy figure.

The mysterious figure stepped into the sunlight. It was a Rockhopper penguin with flashy yellow feathers and gleaming red eyes—Lovelace himself. One by one, the waiting penguins approached Lovelace and offered him a pebble in exchange for answering a question. As a result, Lovelace had

mountains and mountains of pebbles—more than any other penguin in Adelie Land—making it easy for him to impress many females.

As Mumble finally reached the front of the line he noticed a strange set of rings around Lovelace's neck. They looked like the band on the skua's leg!

The Adelies waited breathlessly for Mumble to ask about the lifeless creature deep in the ocean. But Mumble surprised them all by looking Lovelace straight in the eyes and asking, "Were you abducted by Aliens?"

Lovelace stared at Mumble. "*Excuse me?* What kind of question is that?" he asked. "Next!"

"I met a skua with something like that!" Mumble pointed at the rings. "He said he was abducted by Aliens!"

Lovelace puffed up. "This is my Sacred Talisman," he announced. "Bestowed on me by Mystic Beings!"

"Did they have flat faces and no beak?" asked

"The song became love, and love became the egg."

Memphis accidentally drops the egg.

Norma Jean, Mumble, and Memphis are a happy family.

Gloria has a beautiful singing voice.

"Be spontaneous!"

"Can I appeal to your better nature?"

Gloria and Mumble go for a swim with the other penguin graduates.

Adelie Land is like no place Mumble has ever been!

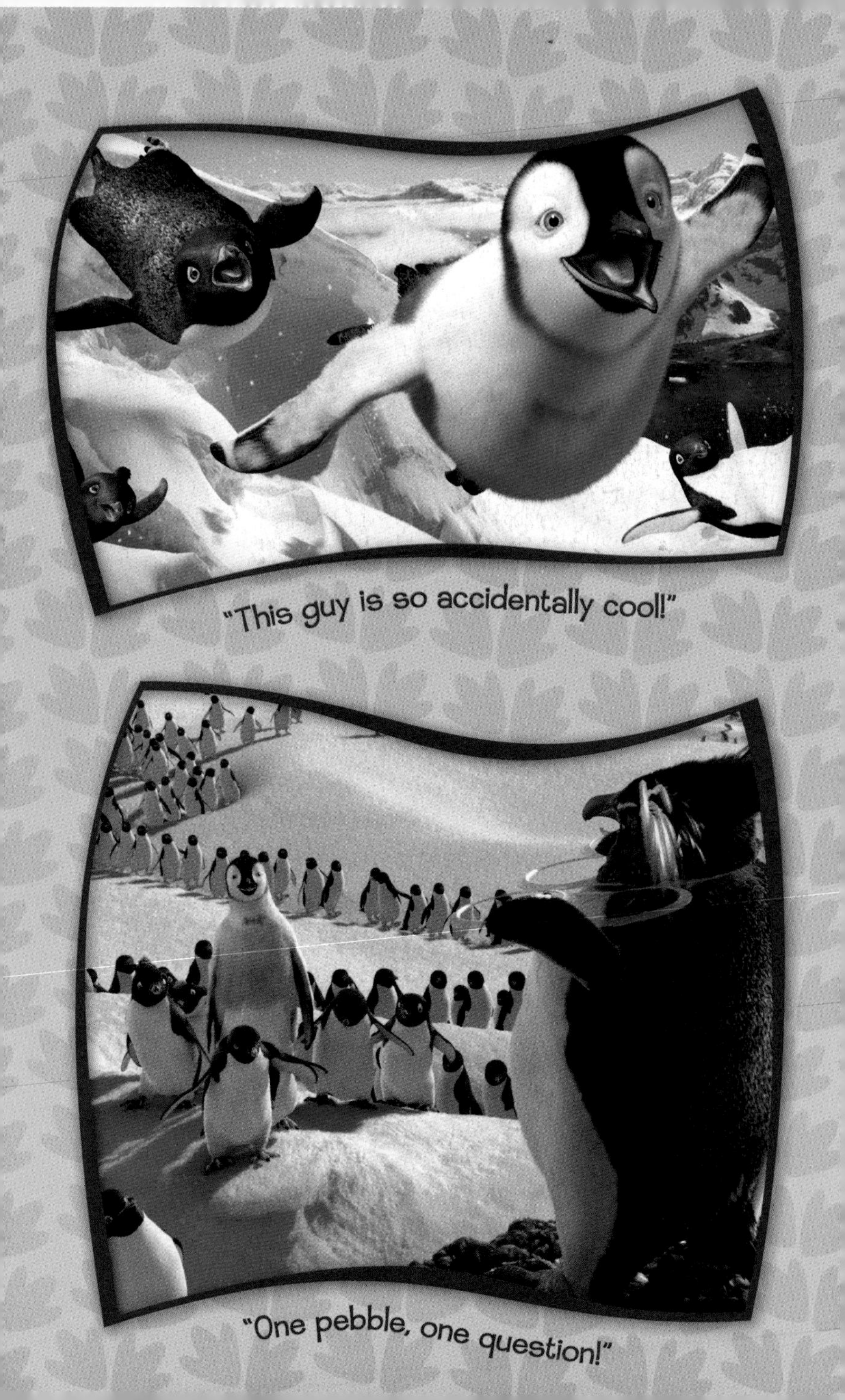
"This guy is so accidentally cool!"

"One pebble, one question!"

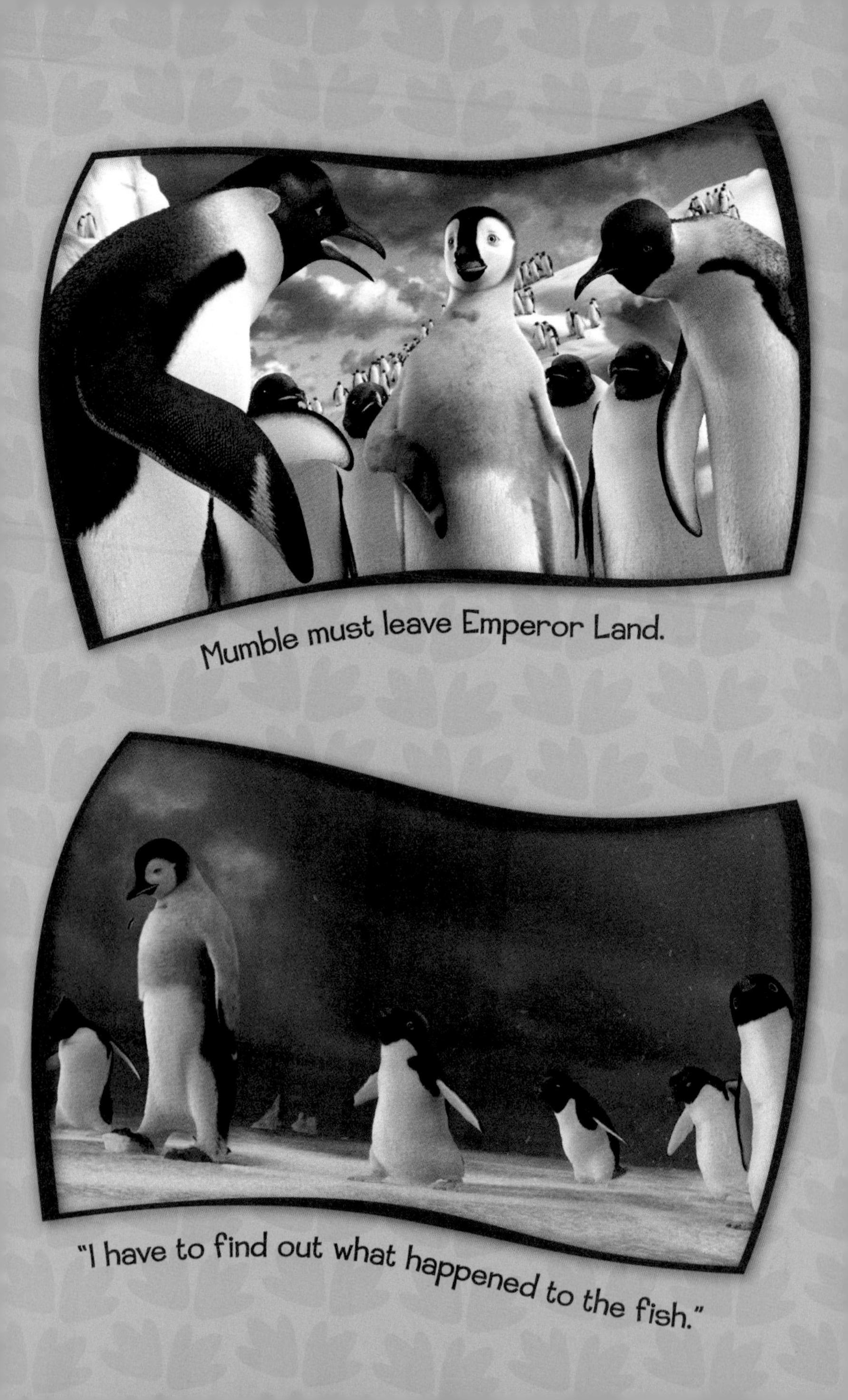

Mumble must leave Emperor Land.

"I have to find out what happened to the fish."

Mumble knows Gloria cannot come with him.

"You're taking our fish!"

TAP-TAP-TAPPITY-TAPPITY-TAP-TAP-TAP!

"I think you better dance now!"

Mumble. "Did they tie you up? Strap you down?"

"One pebble, one question!" snapped Lovelace.

"But you haven't answered any of my questions!" protested Mumble.

"This stranger comes before me and *doubts my powers*?" Lovelace preached. "The Voices are shrieking in my head! No more questions for today!"

"Wait!" Mumble cried.

But Lovelace just turned his back and waddled away, surrounded by female penguins eager for his attention.

"But I have so many questions . . ." Mumble's voice trailed off as Lovelace left.

"You can ask all the questions you want if you get more stones," Ramon said. "You got any stones where you come from?"

"We don't collect stones," replied Mumble.

Rinaldo was confused. "Then how you win the ladies?" he asked.

"Well, we sing," Mumble said.

"You kidding! That's crazy!" laughed the Adelies.

"If someone special likes your song then . . . you know," explained Mumble.

"Oh, and you have someone *especial*—" asked Rinaldo.

"A tall, dark beauty in your romantic past?" interrupted Raul.

"Of whom you never speak?" finished Lombardo.

"Well, there would be," sighed Mumble. "If only I could sing."

"But all birds can sing!" argued Nestor.

Mumble sighed. He knew his friends would only truly understand if they heard his singing for themselves. "LAAAAAA-laaaaaaa-laaaaaaa-LAAAAA!"

"What's he doin'?" asked Lombardo.

"I think he's . . . singing!" replied Raul.

"*Whoa!* I heard an animal once do that, but it turned out he was dead," Ramon said.

"And when she sings, it just about breaks your heart," Mumble sighed. "But my voice is the worst! There's no way we can be together."

"You in tragic shape, man," Ramon said. "Don't worry. We can fix it! You will sing!"

"Really?" asked Mumble, his heart filling with hope. "If I could sing, that would change everything!"

"Jus' do exactly what I say," promised Ramon.

Back in Emperor Land, the mating season was in full bloom. Gloria was easy to find. She was surrounded by male penguins, all trying to impress her with their songs. Suddenly, a new voice carried above the rest. As the voice serenaded her in Spanish, Gloria looked up to see a familiar figure coming toward her. Could it be . . . *Mumble*? But something was not quite right. How had he suddenly learned to sing so well?

"Mumble?" she asked. "Is that really you?"

"Uh . . . hi, Gloria," Mumble stammered. "I mean, *hola*! Do you like my song?"

Before Gloria could reply, she spotted little Ramon hiding behind Mumble's back, singing his heart out. "I would," Gloria said sadly, "if it were really you. Oh, Mumble! How could you fake your Heartsong? That's no way to find a soul mate!"

"Gloria! I . . . I . . ." Mumble gasped as she began to walk away. "I didn't mean to cheat. I just didn't know what else to do!"

But Gloria kept walking, singing her Heartsong in a low, sad voice.

"Gloria!" Mumble desperately called as he leaped onto a mound of ice. "Sing to this!"

Tip-tap-tippity-tappity-tappity-tap!

The rhythm of Mumble's feet tapping on the ice was so catchy that the beat somehow seemed connected to Gloria's own spirit. She couldn't resist singing a few notes back. It filled Mumble with hope. Maybe he *could* win her heart!

TAP-TAP-TAPPITY-TIPPITY-TAPPITY-TAP!

Mumble began to dance like never before. Slowly but surely, his dancing ignited the love in Gloria's song, and she began to sing with all her heart. In that magical moment, the power of their

Heartsongs began to grow, until the music they made was infectious. All across Emperor Land, penguins took notice of Mumble and Gloria, united in song and dance. One by one, they began to join in, and for the very first time, penguins began singing and dancing in perfect harmony. It was the most brilliant moment of Mumble's life!

CHAPTER 7

Mumble and the other penguins were enjoying the dance so much that they failed to notice a dark shadow fall over Emperor Land. Noah the Elder's eyes narrowed as he watched Mumble leading the young penguins. He was certain that this breach of tradition was putting the entire community in grave danger. Noah knew that he had to put a stop to this peculiar behavior at once!

"Stop this unruly nonsense!" his voice boomed across the ice. The penguins stood frozen in place, exchanging guilty glances as their leader reprimanded them. Mumble was the last to stop dancing, causing Noah to focus his wrath on him. "How dare you bring this jiggery-joggery into the heart of our community?" Noah continued, his voice sounding more furious by the moment. He turned to question the other penguins. "Have you all lost your minds?"

"We're just having fun," protested one of the teenage penguins.

"Yeah!" added another. "It's just harmless fun!"

"Harmless?" asked Noah incredulously. "It's this kind of backsliding that has brought the Scarcity upon us!"

"Uh . . . excuse me, Smiley," piped up Ramon. "Can you speak plain penguin, please?"

"He thinks the food shortage has something to do with me," Mumble explained.

Noah turned to Mumble. "Do you not understand that we can only survive here when we are in harmony? You offend the Great Guin! You invite him to withhold his bounty!"

"Wait a minute!" Mumble spoke up. "Happy feet can't cause a famine!"

"If thy unruly display did not cause it, then what did?" asked Eggbert the Elder.

"I think it comes from outside," Mumble said.

"From way beyond the ice. There are things out there—things we don't understand . . ."

"Yeah!" interrupted the Adelies. "Mysteries—mind-boggling mysteries!"

"Aliens," Mumble finished firmly. "There are Aliens, and I hear they're smart. I bet they know what's going on!"

"He's insane!" cried one of the Elders.

"He drove the fish away, and now he's ranting this rubbish," announced Eggbert.

The Adelies tried to defend Mumble—but Eggbert pushed them away with his flipper.

"Let me at him! Let me at him!" yelled Ramon.

"Get your foreign flippers off him!" snapped another Elder as the penguins began to fight.

"And so it follows. Dissent leads to division, and division leads us to doom," Noah said gravely. "You, Mumble Happy Feet, must go! Out to the ice and the wild winds, with no community to shelter you from the cold or the night! You will not bring about our ruin!"

"NO!" screamed Norma Jean. "Don't you take one step, sweetheart. You have as much right to be here as any of these daffy old fools—"

Memphis pushed through the crowd. "Norma Jean!" he interrupted. "I'll deal with this!"

Mumble felt a small surge of hope and pride. He was sure that his father would stand by him at last.

But Memphis turned to him and said, "Mumble, you must renounce your so-called friends, your peculiar thoughts, and your . . . your strange ways. If we are devout and sincere in our praise, the fish will return. You won't have to leave as long as you give up that thing you do with the feet."

"But Pa—" Mumble protested.

"Listen, boy, I was a backslider myself!" Memphis admitted, his voice heavy with regret. "I was careless, and now we're paying the price."

"What's this got to do with Mumble?" Norma Jean asked, confused.

"It's why he is the way he is," replied Memphis.

"But there's nothing *wrong* with him," she protested.

"Face it, Norma Jean!" Memphis said with exasperation. "Our son is all messed up!"

"He is not messed up!" exclaimed Norma Jean. "How can you say that?"

"Because . . ." Memphis paused in agony. "He was just an egg when I *dropped* him!" he finally confessed.

The crowd gasped. At long last, Memphis's terrible secret was out.

"Oh, Memphis," Norma Jean cried, horrified. "Oh, my poor little Mumble!"

"Ma—I'm perfectly fine!" Mumble said, unsure what all the fuss was about.

"No, you're not, boy!" insisted Memphis. "For all our sakes, you must stop this freakishness with the feet!"

"Your father speaks wisely. Heed his suffering heart and repent!" urged Noah.

"But it doesn't make sense," protested Mumble.

"Then your arrogance leaves us no choice!" Noah proclaimed.

"Wait!" Memphis said desperately. "You can do it—it ain't so hard. Please, son, just try—for your mother and me."

Mumble stared at his father for a long moment. "Don't ask me to change, Pa—'cause I can't."

"And that is the end of it!" announced Noah. "You! Begone!"

Mumble was stunned. He had never imagined he would be cast out, or that his own father would ask him to be untrue to himself. If only he could figure out what was causing the famine, Noah wouldn't be able to blame him.

Suddenly Mumble knew what he had to do. As Norma Jean cried out, he said firmly, "No, Ma, it's okay." He turned to Noah and the other Elders. "Let me tell something to you! When I find out what happened to the fish, I'll be back!"

As Mumble, with his head held high, turned to leave, the crowd parted to let him pass.

"Together we prevail," Noah said quietly.

"In the Wisdoms we trust," responded the colony—including Memphis.

"You don't have to go!" Gloria cried. "This isn't fair!"

But Mumble kept walking.

CHAPTER 8

Ramon ran after Mumble. "How you gonna find out what happened to the fish, Tall Guy?"

"Aliens," announced Mumble suddenly. "I'm going to talk to the Aliens."

"How you gonna find Aliens?" asked Lombardo.

"Lovelace," said Mumble, his voice full of determination.

"What?" asked Nestor. "But he don't even like you!"

"That's okay," replied Mumble. "I'll appeal to his better nature."

"How you gonna do that?" Raul asked. "Cruel and unusual punishment?"

"Unimaginable torture?" ventured Lombardo.

"Imaginable torture!" suggested Ramon. "Like your singing!"

"Noooooo!" cried the Adelies in unison.

"Ha, ha," Mumble said sarcastically. "Very funny." Though he pretended to be annoyed, Mumble was secretly very glad that the Amigos were with him. They had already proved to be better, truer friends than he could have ever imagined.

When Mumble and the Adelies reached Lovelace's pebble pile, it was completely deserted. There was no line of penguins waiting to ask questions, no flock of lovestruck females, and—most importantly—no Lovelace. They searched high and low until at last they found Lovelace sprawled behind a mound of stones.

"I have just one question," Mumble said firmly. "And I want a straight answer! Where are the Mystic Beings?"

But Lovelace did not respond.

"Why don't he speak?" asked Nestor. "Lovelace, you okay?"

A long, low gurgling came from Lovelace's throat.

"Aye, he's possessed!" shrieked Nestor.

"It's a seizure! A seizure!" Rinaldo yelled.

Lovelace's eyes bulged as he gasped for air. He used his flipper to point at the rings around his neck.

"No, he's choking!" Mumble realized. "That thing around his neck—it's way too tight!"

The Adelies leaped into action, each one grabbing a ring and pulling with all his might in an attempt to break it. Lovelace gagged and groaned.

"Stop, Amigos, you're hurting him!" exclaimed Mumble. Guiltily, the Adelies let go at once. "Lovelace, how did you get that thing around your neck?" Mumble continued.

"It was bestowed on him! By Mystic Beings!" Nestor spoke up.

But Lovelace shook his head sadly.

"They didn't bestow it?" Mumble asked quietly.

Lovelace was still unable to speak, so he began to tell Mumble about the talisman through funny gestures. Soon Mumble learned that Lovelace had never even met a Mystic Being! The rings had become tangled on his neck while he was swimming along the Forbidden Shore. Mumble started to realize that Lovelace was never a prophet. He was only a fraud. But still, Mumble knew that Lovelace's talisman had come from *somewhere*.

"That thing belongs to the Aliens," Mumble said, pointing at the rings. "If we find them, I bet they could take it off." Mumble didn't say his other thought aloud: that maybe, just maybe, they could also find out what had happened to the fish.

Mumble and the Adelies began the long journey to the Forbidden Shore, with Lovelace trailing behind them. The landscape began to change. There were no cliffs or mountains to break the harsh wind, which carved deep ridges into the icy plain and pushed the penguins back. As they trudged over the ice Mumble and his friends heard a faint voice.

"Mumble!" it called. "Mumble Happy Feet!"

It was Gloria! She had been following their trail since Mumble left Emperor Land.

Mumble was thrilled to see her. "Gloria!" he exclaimed. "What are you doing here?"

Gloria's smile sparkled as she sang a line from her Heartsong, then asked, "Which way, Twinkle Toes?"

For a moment, Mumble felt giddy with happiness as he realized that Gloria, the most popular penguin in Emperor Land, had come after him. But just as quickly, his excitement faded. In his heart, he knew that he couldn't let Gloria follow him. She belonged with the community, where she could lead a normal life—without him.

"No," Mumble said. "Gloria, you can't come with me. You have a life back there. I don't. We could never have an egg out here—"

"I don't need an egg to make me happy," Gloria interrupted. "All I need is *you*."

Mumble could tell his protests weren't having any effect on Gloria. He desperately tried to think of a plan to get her back to Emperor Land. There was no way he would let Gloria become an outcast, too.

"Gloria. It's not you; it's me," he said, trying to sound aloof. "I'm not ready for a serious relationship right now."

"Oh, Mumble," Gloria said. "No matter what you say or do—you're stuck with me! Come on—don't act like you're not totally thrilled that I'm here," she teased.

He tried again. "See, that's your problem. You think you're irresistible—Gloria's so gorgeous, Gloria's so talented . . ." he mocked.

"Excuse me?" Gloria said, surprised.

Then Mumble said the one thing that he knew would drive her away: "Just because you can hit a few high notes—"

"You don't like my singing?" asked Gloria, shocked. She could barely believe what Mumble was saying.

Mumble shrugged. "It's a little showy for my taste. You know—flashy. Froufrou."

"Froufrou?" Gloria asked, wounded. Then the hurt in Gloria's eyes turned to anger, and she pulled herself together. "Ha! That's funny, coming from someone who jigs up and down like a twitchy idiot!"

Mumble started rudely tapping in a frenzy as he stood just inches from Gloria's angry face. "What'd you say? I can't hear you over all that tapping!" he yelled.

"Argh! You stubborn, hippity-hoppity *fool*!" Gloria snapped. She turned her back on Mumble and began the long walk home to Emperor Land.

Mumble's heart sank as he watched Gloria leave. How, in one single day, had he managed to lose everything—his chance to belong in Emperor Land, his family, and now Gloria, too?

"Come on, guys," he sighed. "Let's keep going."

Through the blistering snows of Blizzard Country, through the icy mountains, the penguins traveled. In the Land of the Elephant Seals, they

learned that Alien Annihilators loomed on the Forbidden Shore—terrible machines that could inhale a penguin, seal, or whale and cut them up in an instant. The Adelies stopped joking and chattering, afraid to keep going with Mumble but knowing it would be worse to turn back alone.

Lovelace led them for miles, growing weaker by the hour. His breathing grew shallow, and he often stumbled and fell. A fierce blizzard swirled around them, with winds strong enough to knock the penguins over.

"Oh, man," Raul moaned. "I believe I'm getting cold feet about this."

"Even my cold feet are getting cold feet!" added Rinaldo.

"Come on, guys," Ramon said firmly, his voice nearly drowned out by the howling winds. "Hang in there! Left—right—left—right. Gotta keep going!"

The Adelies formed a huddle with Mumble and Lovelace; together, the penguins were able to withstand the blizzard. When the storm finally passed,

Mumble realized that Lovelace had disappeared. He could see a foreign shape at the bottom of the glacier. Lovelace's tracks led there.

"Look! That's it!" he said to the Adelies. "The Forbidden Shore!"

CHAPTER 9

The Forbidden Shore was a terrible place, littered with hunks of strange objects, sharp hooks, and rusty chains. The penguins walked in the shadows of several buildings that were part of an abandoned whaling station, following Lovelace's tracks in the snow.

"Lovelace? Lovelace!" called Mumble and the Adelies as they searched for the Rockhopper penguin. At last they found him, collapsed against a buoy and struggling to breathe.

"Hang in there, Lovelace!" Mumble said. "I know the Aliens are here somewhere."

"Yeah!" Ramon chimed in. "They wouldn't leave all this stuff behind. Look!" Ramon pointed at the dirty water lapping on the shore. The waves were full of junk—including more Alien rings like the

ones that were choking Lovelace.

"Hey!" yelled Raul as he pointed at the rings. "There's one for each of us!"

Then Lovelace gasped—and stopped breathing! The Adelies crowded around, desperately trying to revive him.

Clang. Clang. Clang.

The ringing of a loud bell echoed through the frosty air. "Help! Please!" yelled Mumble. "We need some help! Help!"

A shadow fell over the group—but it was not help.

It was a huge orca whale leaping out of the water!

"Oh, no," Mumble said. "We've got to—"

Then another orca whale smashed through the ice, separating Mumble, Lovelace, and the Adelies from the mainland! "Whatever you do, stay out of the water!" Mumble yelled.

But Lovelace was too weak. He stumbled off the tiny ice raft, then plunged into the water—with the rings around his neck caught on the buoy's bell!

The heavy bell broke off the buoy and dragged Lovelace deep into the ocean. Mumble plunged in after him as the Adelies scrambled back to the main shore.

It was dark and cold at the bottom of the ocean. Mumble found Lovelace and the bell tangled up with all kinds of junk and trash. He frantically tried to free Lovelace from the rings.

Suddenly Mumble and Lovelace found themselves carried up to the surface of the water. The orcas had found them—and they wanted to play with their prey before eating them! They tossed the penguins back and forth, flinging them through the air at a dizzying pace.

Snap! At long last the rings around Lovelace's neck broke. He was freed! As Lovelace flew through the air, his voice rang out once more: "Rejoice! Rejoice! I found my voice! Been a cheater; been a liar. My purpose now will be much higher!"

"Lovelace! Reach out!" screamed Mumble as the

orcas closed in. He grabbed Lovelace in midair, and the two penguins fell into the sea. They swam to the mainland, barely escaping the orcas' jaws.

Once the penguins were on land, Lovelace turned to the orcas. "You flaccid-finned, overblown baitfish! You're dealing with Lovelace now! Turn round right now! Hightail it back to your mommas!"

The whales plunged back into the sea and silently swam away. The Adelies and Lovelace cheered, but Mumble was suspicious. "Why did they just leave like that? It doesn't make sense," he whispered. "They could have swallowed us in one mouthful."

Then a colossal black shape appeared out of the ghostly fog.

"Not in my wildest dreams . . ." Mumble breathed. "Hey! Hey!"

It was an Alien ship. No wonder the orcas had fled!

"Come on, Fluffy, you know they don't want to chitchat," Ramon said quickly.

"I think they want to be alone," said Rinaldo.

"And we should respect that," added Nestor.

"But this is what we came for," Mumble insisted. "Come on!"

Mumble and the Adelies followed the Alien vessel, racing to the highest point on the glacier, where they saw even more ships gathering on the horizon.

"What are they doing here?" Mumble asked. "It's like they don't even know we exist."

"Let me tell something to you," Ramon said firmly. "This is the end. You did everything penguinly possible."

"You found the Aliens," Lovelace said.

"We gonna testify to that," said Nestor.

"We gonna tell your whole laughing-boy nation that they were dead wrong about you!" the rest of the Adelies chimed in. "Now, let's all go back home! Right now!"

Mumble knew that his friends must return to the safety of their homes. But he had not come so far only to turn back now. And he would not forget the promise he had made back in Emperor Land. He turned to the Adelies.

"Would you make sure Gloria's okay?" he asked. "And my ma. And—if you see Pa, tell him . . . I tried."

"What are you talkin' about?" asked Raul.

"I'm going to find out what's happening to our fish," replied Mumble, staring at the ships. He took a few steps back.

"No!" cried the other penguins in alarm. "What are you doin'?"

"*Adiós, amigos!*" Mumble yelled. And without another word, he jumped over the edge!

Horrified, Lovelace and the Adelies ran to the ledge and watched in shock as Mumble plummeted into the water below.

"*Madre mía!*" Nestor exclaimed. "No penguin could make it through that fall!"

"Look! He's swimmin'!" shouted Ramon, pointing in the direction of the big black ships. He shook his

head in awe. "How tall you think that Tall Boy was?"

"Taller than anyone!" replied Lovelace. "You gonna be a legend, Happy Feet, a tale told for all time!"

CHAPTER 10

But Mumble didn't hear his friends. He swam through the icy water with one goal: to reach the Alien vessel. As he neared the ship he saw a huge net filled with thousands of fish—slowly rising up from the sea!

And in that instant he realized that the Aliens were the ones taking the fish! Mumble was utterly shocked. Never had he imagined that the Aliens were the source of the problem. For the first time in his life, Mumble felt a deep and overpowering sense of anger. He knew that he had to find a way to talk to them—to tell them how much trouble they were causing the penguins.

"Wait!" Mumble yelled. "Stop!" He frantically clamped onto the net with his beak and was lifted out of the water. Aliens aboard the ship poked

at him with long poles, but Mumble held on fast. Another Alien jabbed hard at Mumble, then another, and he finally fell into the water. The ship's engines rumbled to a start, and its huge propellers started spinning. Millions of tiny bubbles blinded Mumble. When the churning waters quieted, the Alien ship was far away.

Mumble followed the Alien vessel, heading straight for the rough seas of open water. He was determined to make the Aliens understand that the penguins needed the fish to survive.

The mountainous waves crashed onto Mumble. He was only able to resurface long enough to watch the ships sail farther into the distance. Still Mumble tried to follow the Alien ships, though he spent more time underwater than above. One after another, the waves pushed him down. Mumble gasped for air and tried to swim a little farther. Darkness swirled around him—he could see; he could swim; he could breathe no more.

Unconscious, Mumble was carried to the shore

by the waves. Among the trash and the slippery pools of spilled oil lay a motionless creature: Mumble Happy Feet.

Mumble would not remember the flashing headlights, the roar of the truck, or the gentle hands that lifted him off the shore. When he woke up, he was in a tunnel filled with bright, blinding light. Mumble tried to figure out where he was. He walked toward the light and found himself in a place that looked like home . . . but not quite.

"What is this place?" Mumble asked.

"You're in heaven, friend. Penguin heaven," replied a dazed-looking penguin nearby.

"Is it near Emperor Land?" asked Mumble, confused.

"It's wherever you want it to be," the zombie penguin replied.

Mumble started walking toward an ice shelf. *Bang!* He had walked right into a wall! The snow,

the ice—almost everything around him—was fake.

"Try the water. It's really real," suggested the zombie penguin. But Mumble just shook his head. Where was he—and what was going on?

Then Mumble noticed an Alien watching him. It looked exactly as he had imagined: a big ugly penguin with a flabby face and no beak!

"Why are you taking our fish?" Mumble demanded. "We can't survive without them!"

But the Alien just walked away.

"No! Wait!" cried Mumble. Then he noticed dozens more Aliens—all watching him. Mumble cleared his throat. "Hello! Hello from Emperor Land! I'm sure you don't mean to, but you're causing us an awful lot of grief. You're kind of killing us out there!"

No one responded.

"Am I not making myself clear?" Mumble shouted. "Can anyone hear me? Does anyone understand? I'm speaking plain Penguin! Talk to me!"

But it was no use. No one bothered to listen to the squawking penguin in the zoo.

After three days, Mumble lost his voice. After three weeks, he almost lost his mind. Every day, Aliens stared at him, and more fish rained down on him than any one penguin could eat. But all Mumble saw were visions of those he had loved most—hungry, waiting for him to return, waiting for him to help them. More than anything, Mumble wanted to share the fish with all the visions he saw—but they were just illusions. He was utterly alone.

Mumble Happy Feet—son of Memphis and Norma Jean, sweetheart of Gloria, and true Amigo—had finally lost all of himself.

And his story would have ended there if not for . . .

Tap. Tap. Tap.

Mumble was lost in a daze, but he heard the sound and wondered what it was. He shook his head and looked around.

A little Alien was watching him. She tapped on the glass again, trying to get his attention.

Tap. Tap. Tap.

Something stirred in Mumble. A long-sleeping memory, a sense of who he was, began to awake. His foot gently, slowly began to move.

Tap. Tap. Tap.

An old, familiar rhythm swelled in Mumble's soul as the sounds of his Heartsong came to life.

Tap-tap-tappity-tippity-tap!

Mumble's feet moved faster. The little Alien grinned and tapped the rhythm back to him.

TAP-TAP-TAPPITY-TIPPITY-TAP-TAP-TAP!

Mumble was back—and dancing better than ever!

More and more Aliens began to notice Mumble's amazing tapping. They clapped and laughed with delight. After weeks of trying, Mumble had finally found a way to reach them!

"He's communicating with us," an Alien said. "We tap—he answers! Where on earth did you find this creature?"

"He washed up on a beach, all the way from

Antarctica!" replied another Alien.

"What if he's not alone? We've got to return him to his natural habitat!" added another.

Mumble didn't know exactly what the Aliens were saying. It was enough for him to know that he had gotten through to them—and that maybe, just maybe, he could make them understand, and finally be able to keep his promise to the penguins back home.

CHAPTER 12

Back in Emperor Land, the food shortage problem kept getting worse. The penguins were weak from lack of nourishment. Hopelessness and despair had spread through the colony. There was not much to do—and even less to say—about the terrible situation they were in. The Emperor penguins were so lost in their sadness that they didn't even notice the tiny figure hippity-hopping along the horizon, heading straight for them.

Then they heard a voice carried on the frosty air. "Hey! Hello!" it called.

The Emperor penguins looked up. They did not recognize the sleek and well-fed penguin approaching them.

"Isn't that the fellow with the wacky feet?" one asked.

"Looks like it," another penguin replied. "I thought he was dead."

"Hey, everybody!" Mumble yelled as he stood on an ice rise looking over the group. "Listen up! I've got big news! I found out who's taking the fish. It's the Aliens! I made contact with them!"

The crowd of penguins didn't believe him. "Yeah, right," one of them taunted. "The old lunatic is back."

"Someone get Noah!" another one exclaimed.

"Mumble? Is that you?" someone asked.

Mumble's heart leaped. He knew that voice.

"Gloria!" Mumble exclaimed. His voice fell when he noticed all the chicks gathered at her feet. Mumble was crushed by the thought that Gloria was taken. He tried to sound normal. "So—which one's yours?" he asked, pointing to the chicks.

"All of them," she replied. "This is my singing class. I've been teaching the blues."

"So you're not—" Mumble began.

"I guess I never heard the right song . . ."

Gloria's voice trailed off.

"Th-that's great news!" he exclaimed, thrilled that he might have a chance with Gloria. "I mean, I found out who's taking the fish! And they're coming here! Oh, Gloria, the things they can do! And . . . and they're coming here!"

"Oh, is that so?" Gloria said. Mumble could tell she was just humoring him.

"What's coming? Where? When?" asked the other penguins anxiously.

"The Aliens! They'll be here soon! I think they really want to help us!" Mumble said excitedly.

"So now you speak to them?" Gloria asked as her eyes widened.

"Well, they don't speak Penguin," Mumble explained. "But they seem to respond to this." Mumble showed them a few fancy steps.

Tap-tap-tappity-tappity-tap!

A cluster of hungry penguins formed around Mumble. "We're starving, and you expect us to do this jiggery-jog?" one of them yelled angrily.

"You've got to be crazy!" complained one of the penguins.

"No way. I'm not doing that," another snapped.

"We should all do it," Mumble said enthusiastically. "It really gets their attention!"

Tap-tap-tappity-tappity-tap!

"So!" a voice boomed across the ice. "You dare to come back!"

The crowd parted to reveal Noah and the other Elders charging across the ice, ready to confront Mumble.

"He says he's found Aliens, and they're taking our fish!" a young penguin said excitedly. "He says that they're coming, and all we have to do to get more fish is dance!" The little penguin tried to tap-dance.

"There no be such thing as Aliens!" Noah thundered before being interrupted by an unfamiliar sound.

Beep! Beep! Beep!

"Uh . . . Mumble," Gloria said. "Turn around."

On Mumble's back was a blinking computer chip. The penguins had never seen anything like it.

"He's got a disease!" one of them cried. "Stay back!"

"No, no, no," Mumble said. "Don't be afraid. The Aliens gave it to me. I think it's a way for them to find me."

"You led them here?" Noah asked, outraged. "You turned them on your own kind?"

"Wait a minute!" Gloria exclaimed. "You just said there was no such thing as Aliens!"

"Well . . . there's not!" Noah stammered. "But if there were, only a traitorous lunatic would bring them here!"

"But they have to come!" Mumble insisted. "They're the ones taking our fish. They're the only ones who can do something about it!"

"Only the Great Guin has the power to give and take away," Noah preached.

"But the Great Guin didn't put things out of whack. The Aliens did!" argued Mumble.

"Beware the rantings of a fool!" Noah shouted. "For what a fool believes, no reason hath the power to reason away. So what you all must ask yourselves today is: Who is the fool here?"

There was a moment of silence as the penguins tried to decide what to do. They looked from Noah to Mumble and then back to Noah. Then one of the teenagers turned to Mumble. "How does that thing with the feet go?" he asked.

"Oh, it's easy!" Mumble assured him. "Just do this."

Tap-tap-tappity-tippity-tap!

A few more penguins began trying to tap. Noah and the other Elders grew more upset. "Together we prevail. In the wisdoms we trust!" they chanted, using the phrases that had always worked to hold the group together.

As more penguins joined Mumble in dance Noah screamed over their tapping. "We call upon you, Almighty Guin! Forgive those who befoul our community!"

Far away, in a lonely ice cave, Norma Jean heard the commotion. The familiar sound of tapping—could it possibly be that Mumble had returned? Norma Jean hurried to the heart of Emperor Land and pushed through the crowd, with the Adelies right behind her. "My baby boy is back!" she cried.

"Mama!" Mumble exclaimed as he rushed to give Norma Jean a hug. Mother and son danced together in joy, surrounded by Gloria and the excited Amigos.

But Mumble knew there was one more thing he had to do. "Where's Pa?" he asked, searching for his father in the huge crowd of dancing penguins.

"Your pa is . . ." Norma Jean's voice trailed off. "Come and I'll show you."

Mumble followed her to an ice cave. He saw a shadow move inside it. "Pa?" Mumble called. "I've come back, Pa!"

A sad, slumped figure came out of the cave. It was Memphis. "Son? Is it truly you?" he asked.

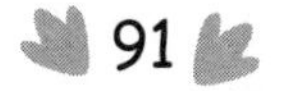

"Every last bit of me," Mumble replied.

"Dance for him, Memphis!" urged Norma Jean.

But Memphis just shook his head. "Oh, he don't need me."

"Come on, Pa—it's the easiest thing in the world," Mumble explained. "It's just like singing with your body. *See?*" Mumble showed Memphis a few simple steps.

"You'll have to forgive me, boy. The music's gone clean out of me," Memphis said quietly.

"No it hasn't!" insisted Mumble. "It's just one big old foot in front of the other. Try!"

Memphis wasn't sure where to start, but he followed Mumble's example. As he moved his feet a warm feeling stretched up his legs, into his body, and straight into his heart. He began to relax and enjoy the movement. "Oooh. Well, that feels good. Yeah—I like it!" Memphis's heart was light once more as he danced with his son in perfect harmony.

And then: *chuppa-chuppa-chop-chop-chop-chuppa-chuppa*! A deafening noise drowned out all other sounds—even the penguins' tapping. A strange black creature appeared from the heavens, hovering above Emperor Land, slicing the sky with its blades.

The Aliens had arrived!

Noah and the other Elders watched the helicopter with wide eyes, finally realizing that the funny penguin with the strange walk had been right. In the face of such an overwhelming sight, they could no longer deny Mumble's truth. All of the Emperor penguins knew that this was their only chance to save themselves.

The helicopter landed at the top of a high cliff. Aliens came out of it and walked onto the ice. The Emperor penguins turned to Noah, and Noah turned to Mumble.

"Son," Memphis said, "I think you better dance now!"

And in front of the entire Penguin Nation, Mumble started up a new rhythm. His family joined him, then ten more penguins, then a hundred, then a thousand, then tens of thousands! Surrounded by his community, all of them following his lead on every step, Mumble finally, totally, and completely belonged. He tapped a rhythm and faced the Aliens.

And the Aliens clapped the rhythm right back!

"It's working!" Mumble yelled. "Keep dancing!"

Later that day, the Aliens got into their helicopter and returned to their homeland—bringing with them video of the amazing dancing penguins. The penguins, of course, would never know that the Aliens were actually human scientists who presented their story to a World Congress.

When the viewing of the video footage was over, the chairman asked, "What could it be? I've never seen *anything* like those penguins."

"Some kind of neurological disorder?" suggested an expert. "Perhaps a nutritional deficiency?"

"Are you saying this deserves a long-term study?" asked the chairman.

"Oh, absolutely," replied a delegate. "This footage has gone all over the world."

"But what about the illegal factory ships?" asked another delegate.

All the scientists and delegates looked to the chairman. "Look at those little toe-tappers go," he marveled. "We'll tell all those clowns to get their fleets outta there!"

A scientist pointed to a map. "A no-fishing zone here, and here, should help their numbers bounce back up nicely," she explained. "And a ban on all fishing in the area!"

"The sheriff's here and he's banging up the sign," announced the chairman. "NO FISHING!"

And so it was that the Aliens, who had once caused such hardship to the penguins, were now able to help them. Within months, the water around Emperor Land was full of fish. The penguins soon grew sleek and strong again. If you visit that snow-covered land, you will find them dancing

still, the songs of their hearts and the dances of their souls merging to make a glorious harmony. You may even see Mumble and Gloria dancing together, as they were always meant to do. And if you listen very carefully, amid all the *tap-tap-tippity-tap* and *bang-boom-bang* and *boom-boom-sssssssshhhh* and *chippita-chippita-whishhhhhhhhhh,* you will hear the penguins calling out the name of the one penguin who was brave enough, and true enough, to follow his heart no matter where it would lead.

"MUMBLE!"